Harriet walked into the middle of the circle. It was big, perhaps twenty metres across, and all the corn in it was squashed down to the ground, flat, as though an enormously heavyweight had rested there.

As she stood there now, in the stillness, with no sound but distant birdsong, a hare suddenly came out into the corn circle and stopped and sat up. It turned its head a little sideways, the better to see her.

Harriet stood stock-still. Aren't you handsome, she thought, with your tawny coat and your black-tipped ears and your long hind legs. Don't run away. I won't hurt you.

For a moment the hare stayed where it was, watching her. Then, to her great surprise, it lolloped right up to her . . .

D1340823

Titles available by award-winning author, and creator of *Babe*,
DICK KING-SMITH

Published by Corgi Pups
Happy Mouseday★

Published by Young Corgi
All Because of Jackson
Connie and Rollo
E.S.P.
The Guard Dog★
Horse Pie
Omnibombulator
The Dick King-Smith Collection
(includes **E.S.P.**, **The Guard Dog** and **Horse Pie**)

Published by Doubleday/Corgi Yearling
A Mouse Called Wolf
Mr Ape
Billy the Bird

Published by Corgi
Dirty Gertie Mackintosh illustrated by Ros Asquith
Godhanger
The Crowstarver

★Also available in book and audio tape packs.

HARRIET'S HARE

Dick King-Smith

ILLUSTRATED BY
VALERIE LITTLEWOOD

CORGI YEARLING BOOKS

HARRIET'S HARE
A CORGI YEARLING BOOK : 0 440 86340 6

First published in Great Britain by Doubleday,
a division of Transworld Publishers

PRINTING HISTORY
Doubleday edition published 1994
Corgi Yearling edition published 1996

13 15 17 19 20 18 16 14

Corgi Yearling Books are published by Transworld Publishers,
61–63 Uxbridge Road, London W5 5SA,
a division of The Random House Group Ltd,
in Australia by Random House Australia (Pty) Ltd,
20 Alfred Street, Milsons Point, Sydney, NSW 2061, Australia,
in New Zealand by Random House New Zealand Ltd,
18 Poland Road, Glenfield, Auckland 10, New Zealand
and in South Africa by Random House (Pty) Ltd,
Endulini, 5a Jubilee Road, Parktown 2193, South Africa.

Printed and bound in Great Britain by
Cox & Wyman Ltd, Reading, Berkshire.

CONTENTS

Chapter One

Harriet sat up, suddenly wide-awake. Whatever was that noise?

It was a rushing, tearing, swishing noise – just the sound a rocket makes on Guy Fawkes Night, yet much much louder. But this was the start of a midsummer day and – she looked at her watch – early too, not five o'clock yet.

She leaped out of bed and ran to the window.

The farmhouse and its buildings were tucked into the side of a gentle hill, and in the little flat valley below were two large fields, the nearer one green, the further one gold.

In the first, her father's cows would normally have been waiting around the gateway for him to come and fetch them in for morning milking. But now the whole herd was galloping and buck-jumping around the pasture as though something had scared the wits out of them.

The second field was of wheat, almost ready for harvesting, that looked from the house above like a square golden blanket, glowing in the morning sunlight. But there seemed to be a hole in the blanket. In one corner of the wheatfield,

Harriet could see, there was a perfect circle of flattened corn.

It took Harriet a quarter of an hour to dress and slip out of the house and run down the dewy hillside. By now the cows had quietened, and she ran through them to the wheatfield beyond, climbed over its gate and pushed through the standing corn to step into that perfect circle.

What had made it? What had made the noise that had woken her and terrified the cows? Whatever had happened in the field called Ten Acre on Longhanger Farm at the start of this July day?

Harriet walked into the middle of the circle. It was big, perhaps twenty metres across, and all the corn in it was squashed down to the ground, flat, as though an

 enormously heavy weight
had rested there.

As she stood there now,
in the stillness, with no
sound but distant birdsong,
a hare suddenly came out

into the corn circle and stopped and sat up. It turned its head a little sideways, the better to see her.

Harriet stood stock-still. Aren't you handsome, she thought, with your tawny coat and your black-tipped ears and your long hind legs. Don't run away. I won't hurt you.

For a moment the hare stayed where it was, watching her. Then, to her great surprise, it lolloped right up to her.

Surprise is one thing, but total amazement is quite another, and that was what Harriet next felt when all of a sudden the hare said, loudly and clearly, 'Good morning.'

Harriet pinched herself, hard. Wake up, she thought. This whole thing is a dream, hares don't talk, and then she said it aloud: 'Hares don't talk.'

'I'm sure they don't as a general rule,' said the hare, 'but I'm a rather unusual hare.'

'You certainly are,' said Harriet. 'Are you anything to do with this corn circle?'

For a moment the hare didn't answer but fell to grooming its face. Then it said, 'What's your name?'

'Harriet.'

'Can you keep a secret, Harriet?'

'Yes.'

'I,' said the hare, 'am a visitor from outer space.'

'You mean . . . this circle was made by your spacecraft?'

'Yes.'

'So you come from another planet?'

'Yes. I come from Pars.'

'Pars?' said Harriet. 'Is that near Mars?'

'Oh no,' said the hare. 'Much much further away.'

'But,' said Harriet, 'I thought that aliens were . . . well, little green men with four arms and eyes on stalks.'

'Not far wrong,' said the hare. 'But you see, Harriet, we Partians have the ability to change. Imagine how strange your modern world here would seem to a caveman. Whatever would he make of microsurgery and satellite television and supersonic flight? You have to understand that on Pars we are as far ahead of you people on Earth as you are now ahead of the cavemen. One of the things we can do, for example, is to speak all earthly languages. But perhaps to you our most astonishing skill is that we have perfected the ability to change our shapes. When my colleagues left me here in this cornfield, I could, for instance, have decided to become a tiger (though that might have caused a bit of a stir in deepest Wiltshire) or a dog or a sheep or anything else you like. But I chose to change myself into a hare.'

'Why?' asked Harriet.

'Because in this world the hare has always been thought to be a beast of magic. People said that hares were witches and could melt away and reappear, to dance and play in the light of the moon. (Incidentally some still say that if you look at the full moon, it is not a man's face that you see there, but the shape of a hare.) And others believed that hares could change their sex at will.'

'Oh,' said Harriet. 'Which are you at the moment?'

'I,' said the hare, 'am a buck and fully intend to remain so, for the length of my stay on Earth.'

Harriet felt suddenly dreadfully disappointed. Here she was, in her father's wheatfield, deep in conversation with a magic hare, but perhaps he would only be around for a very short time.

'How long are you staying?' she said.

'It depends,' said the hare, 'on how much I like it here. This is actually my first Earth holiday.'

'You've come here for a holiday?' asked Harriet.

'Oh yes,' said the hare.

'Everyone on Pars takes a holiday abroad every so often. Interplanetary travel is so quick and easy nowadays, you know – to anywhere in the solar system that you fancy. I've been to a number of heavenly bodies but never to Earth. I just fancied going somewhere quite different this year, somewhere rather primitive, where the technology was not very far advanced and one could relax among the simple, ignorant natives. So I came here. But that's enough about me, Harriet. Tell me a bit about yourself. All I know is your name.'

'Well,' said Harriet, 'I'm nearly eight and I go to the village school, and my dad's a farmer and we've got cows and some sheep and some chickens, and Dad works the farm all by himself except sometimes he gets a relief milker in so that we can have a bit of a holiday.'

'But your mother helps with the animals, I expect?' said the hare.

'My mother's dead,' said Harriet. 'She died when I was quite little. I don't really remember her. But I help Dad. I look after the hens, and I feed the calves, and this year I bottled three lambs. They'd lost their mother too.'

'You like animals,' said the hare.

'Oh yes. Specially my pony. She's a strawberry roan, twelve and a half hands. She's called Breeze. By the way, I don't know your name.'

'Nor do I,' said the hare, 'if you see what I mean. On Pars I had a perfectly good name, but I really haven't given a thought about what to be called now that I am a specimen of *Lepus europaeus occidentalis*.'

'What?'

'Latin name for a hare.'

'You speak Latin too?'

'I told you. Partians are omnilingual.'

'Oh,' said Harriet. 'Well, what am I going to call you?'

'Whatever you like,' said the hare. 'You choose.'

Harriet thought.

A visitor from outer space that speaks all languages, that can transform itself into any shape, a creature of witchcraft, a magician. He's a wizard, that's what he is.

'Wiz,' she said.

The hare, who had remained sitting in the middle of the corn circle throughout the whole of this conversation, stood up on his long hind legs. His ears raised, his large brown eyes enquiring, he looked the very picture of astonishment.

'Wiz?' he said.

'Yes. That's what I shall call you.'

'Oh, very well,' sighed Harriet's hare. 'Wiz it is.'

Chapter Two

Suddenly a dog barked. Harriet
turned to see her father coming
down the hill towards the cow
pasture, the old sheepdog, Bran,
running ahead of him.

Bran's barking said quite clearly,
today as every day, 'Come along,
you silly cows, whatever you're
doing – it's time for milking.' And
as soon as the farmer opened the

gate, Bluebell, the master cow whose right it was to be first through any gate, began the climb up the trackway through the home paddock, the rest of the herd following behind her.

'That's my dad,' said Harriet, but she found she was talking to herself, for the hare had vanished.

She climbed back over the gate of the wheatfield and ran towards her father.

'Hattie!' he called in astonishment. 'What in the world are you doing out so early?'

Harriet thought quickly.

'Can you keep a secret?' Wiz had said. She must say nothing about him.

'There's a corn circle, Dad!' she cried. 'In our wheat. I saw it from my bedroom window.'

Leaving Bran to take the cows on up the hill, the farmer walked back with her to the cornfield.

'I've heard about these, Hattie,' he said, 'but I've never seen one, except in photos.'

'What made it, Dad, d'you think?'

'There are lots of theories. Some say badgers, rolling in the corn, but it would have taken a hundred giant badgers to make this. Most likely it's caused by a kind of whirling vortex of wind, like a tornado. Though of course there are always the nutters who say that corn circles are made by spacecraft!'

'That's rubbish,' said Harriet.

'It is!' said her father.

Somewhere in the standing corn there was a rustling noise.

'Rabbit in there,' said Harriet's father.

'Or a hare perhaps?' said Harriet.

'Could be. They'd better be out of it before I put the combine in.'

He takes his gun with him when he rides the combine, Harriet thought. I must warn Wiz.

'When will this field be fit, Dad, d'you think?' she asked.

Her father pulled off an ear of wheat, rubbing it between his hands to free the kernels and then chewing them to test their ripeness.

'Not long now,' he said.

From the top of the hill, Bran barked. Again there was no mistaking his meaning: 'The cows are in the yard. I've done my bit, so what d'you expect me to do now – milk 'em?'

'Come on, Hattie,' said her father. 'I've got work to do.'

'So have I,' said Harriet. 'I'm

going to load the washing-machine before I start getting your breakfast. And the downstairs wants dusting.'

'I'd forgotten,' said her father. 'It's the start of your school summer holidays, isn't it?'

'Yes,' said Harriet, 'but there's a lot of work to be done.'

Poor girl, thought her father as he let the first cows into the milking-parlour. She's had to grow up fast without a mother. Though I think she's mostly forgotten her now. Which I never shall. I just worry that it's not much fun for Hattie, stuck here alone with me. What she needs is a bit of magic in her life. Children believe in magic. She probably thinks that corn circle was made by extra-terrestrials. Load of rubbish.

Later that morning, when the washing was in the drier and she had flicked a duster about (a woman from the village came twice a week to do the cleaning), Harriet went back down to the corn circle. She half expected to see Wiz waiting for her, but the circle was empty. Where had he gone? When would she see him again? *Would* she see him again? Like her, he was on holiday, but the fact that *she* was staying here, on Longhanger Farm, didn't mean that *he* was. He could go wherever he liked.

She trudged back across the cow pasture. He might be miles away by now, loping across the downs, simply enjoying being a hare, with no thought for her at all.

Just then she saw, not five metres away, a brown shape squatting motionless in a clump of grass, long ears flat to its head.

'Wiz!' she cried, and at the sound of her voice the hare leaped up from its form and sped away.

'Come back!' called Harriet, but to no avail, and she felt the prick of tears as the animal disappeared through the nearest hedge. He didn't want to have anything more to do with her. Never again would she speak with the magical visitor from Pars. Or maybe, thought Harriet, I'm going potty and I just imagined it all.

'Wrong hare,' said a voice behind her.

'Oh, Wiz!' cried Harriet. 'Am I glad to see you! I was beginning to wonder . . .' She stopped.

'If you'd dreamed the whole thing?' said the hare.

'Yes . . . no . . . I didn't know what to think.'

'Did you tell your father about me?'

'No. I promised not to. But Wiz, you must be careful, because soon he'll be harvesting the wheat and that means he goes round and round the field on a big machine called a combine, and he shoots any rabbit that runs out, specially at the end when there's only a little square of corn left in the middle. People eat rabbits, you see.'

'But I'm not a rabbit.'

'Hares too,' said Harriet.

'People eat *hares*?' said Wiz.

'I'm afraid so. Jugged hare is very good.'

'Jugged?'

'Yes. Cut up in bits and stewed with wine and herbs. Sorry, but they do.'

'How primitive!' said Wiz. 'So bad for you, all this meat-eating. How fortunate that I chose to become a hare and not a tiger. Your grass is really excellent.'

'Are you all vegetarians on Pars?' asked Harriet.

'Absolutely. No-one kills anything for food.'

'But what about wars? People here on Earth are always killing one another.'

'So pointless,' said Wiz. 'You really are still like savages. We Partians like to live as long as possible. Admittedly we haven't yet cracked the riddle of everlasting life, but we like to reckon on a couple of hundred years or so apiece before we're bottled.'

'Bottled?'

'We don't bury bodies or burn them like you barbarians,' said the hare. 'We preserve our dead in a special solution. Standing upright, in bottles.'

'They must be very big bottles,' said Harriet.

'No. We're very small people. All you need is a couple of shelves and you can keep all your ancestors. You never really lose anyone.'

How horrible, thought Harriet. She felt suddenly angry.

'I lost my mum, remember?' she said.

'I'm so sorry, Harriet,' said the hare. 'I do apologize – I wasn't thinking what I was saying. Too fond of the sound of my own voice, that's my trouble. Will you forgive me?'

Harriet nodded.

'You didn't mean any harm,' she muttered.

'On the contrary,' said Wiz, 'I should like to do you some good. Perhaps I'll be able to, one of these fine days. And talking of fine days, I must remember to watch out for your father on his combine. I want to get back to Pars in one piece.'

'Yes,' said Harriet, 'you must be careful, Wiz. It isn't only Dad. You might meet a poacher with a gun or with dogs, or a fox might get you in the night, or you might be run over on the roads.'

'Good heavens!' said the hare. 'Maybe I should have been a tiger after all.'

'I'm glad you're not,' said Harriet, and she knelt down and stroked the hare's tawny back.

'I'm sorry I snapped at you, Wiz,' she said.

'I deserved it,' said the hare.

'We're friends again, aren't we?'
Harriet said.

'Certainly,' said Wiz. 'You are
literally my one and only friend on
Earth.'

He stood up on his hind legs and,
turning his head slightly to one
side, gazed up the hill towards the
farmhouse.

'Eyes on the sides of one's head
are a nuisance,' he said. 'We
Partians have three hundred and
sixty degrees sight – stalk-eyed,

you know – and even you humans have binocular vision. But a hare, it seems, doesn't see straight ahead too well. Which is your bedroom?'

'The right-hand one of the three upper windows,' said Harriet. 'That's mine.'

'I might come up and pay you a visit some time,' said Wiz.

'But how? Hares can't climb up walls.'

'I'm an unusual hare.'

'Well, for goodness sake don't let Dad catch sight of you, or our dog, Bran.'

'They won't see me,' said Wiz, 'but I'll be seeing you,' and he lolloped away across the field.

Chapter Three

For a couple of days Harriet saw
nothing of Wiz.

From her window she could spot
the occasional rabbit in the valley
below, but she saw no hare,
European or Partian. She rode over
the farm on Breeze, now and again
calling, 'Wiz! Wiz!' but no-one
answered.

'Wish you could talk like he

34

does,' she said to the pony. 'We could have ever such interesting conversations,' and Breeze blew a bubbly snort of agreement.

'At least,' said Harriet, 'I can tell you all about Wiz. That's not breaking my promise to him, because although you can understand a lot of things I say, I doubt if a magic hare from outer space would mean much to you. And I can't talk about it to Dad, or Mrs Wisker the cleaning lady, or the postman, or the vet, and I haven't got a mum to tell even if I could. I wish I did – have a mum, I mean. It must be nice.'

That evening, when her father came up to say good-night to her, Harriet said 'Dad. D'you think you'll ever get married again?'

Her father sat down on the bed.

'Would you be pleased if I did, Hattie?' he said.

'Well, yes, I suppose so. If it was someone you liked.'

'Only liked?'

'Well, loved then.'

Harriet's father took hold of her hand and with one finger idly tickled the palm of it, just as he used to when she was little and he played 'Round and round the garden like a teddy bear' with her.

'I don't honestly think it's very likely,' he said. 'Just because Mummy's not here any more doesn't mean I've stopped loving her. And anyway, I don't meet anybody much, do I?'

'No.'

'I don't like to think of you being lonely.'

'I'm not a bit lonely,' said

Harriet. 'I've got you and Breeze and Bran and all the other animals.'

She yawned.

'And Wiz,' she said sleepily.

'Who's Wiz?' said her father.

'Oh,' said Harriet. 'Oh . . . that's my nickname for Mrs Wisker.'

Mrs Wisker was a stout middle-aged widow, a thorough cleaner but not the world's fastest worker.

'Funny name for her,' said Harriet's father. 'You don't call her that to her face, do you?'

'Oh no,' said Harriet. 'She might not like it. But I like her – she's nice isn't she?'

'Perhaps I'd better marry her then?'

'Oh, Dad!'

That night, Harriet dreamed about Wiz. He had somehow climbed up to her bedroom window and come in.

When she woke, she got out of bed and leaned on the windowsill to scan the valley below, but it was hareless.

There was a house martin's nest in the eaves just over her window, and she watched one of the parent birds returning from hawking insects. It swooped up with a beakful, just a metre or so away from her face, and she could hear the cheeping of the hungry youngsters in their cup-shaped nest of mud above.

As the martin wheeled away again, a sparrow fluttered out of the creeper on the house wall and landed on the sill, right beside Harriet, and chirped at her.

'Cheeky thing!' she said,

expecting it to fly off at the sound of her voice so close. But instead it flew past her into the room.

Harriet turned round, to see the hare sitting up on the bedroom carpet. Of the sparrow there was no sign.

'Wiz!' cried Harriet. 'How on earth did you get here?'

'Not so much *on* earth as *off* earth!' said the hare. 'I flew.'

'You were that sparrow? You changed into it?'

'And back again, I'm glad to say. I don't think I much fancy being *Passer domesticus*.'

'More Latin?'

'Yes.'

'But you'll have to fly out again. You can't just jump out of the window.'

'True. But next time I think I'll

be a less ordinary bird. In the
meantime, how are you, Harriet?'

'Quite well, thank you,' said
Harriet. 'And you?'

'I'm really rather enjoying my
holiday on Earth,' said Wiz. 'It's a
lovely bit of country, up here on
the Wiltshire Downs. Very
different from Pars.'

'What's Pars like?' asked Harriet.

'Absolutely flat. Not a hump nor
a hollow anywhere. That's why I
like it here. And I like being a hare
too – it's fun. We Partians are slow
movers, but now I can run like the
wind.'

'Have you come across any other
hares?' said Harriet.

'Since you ask, Harriet,' said
Wiz, 'I did meet a rather attractive
young doe.'

'Did you speak to her?'

'Of course.'

'Not in English?'

'No. In Leporine.'

'Oh. So you can speak animal languages as well?'

'Certainly.'

In the yard below, Bran barked.

Harriet looked out of the window to see her father and the dog setting out to fetch the herd for milking.

'Well then, what's Bran saying?' she asked.

'He's saying a number of things,' said the hare. 'One is a message to the cows, that he's on his way. One is a greeting to your father, that he's glad to be with him. And one is just a general expression of well-being: "It's a lovely morning and I'm a healthy, happy old dog who's glad to be alive!"'

'You can't tell all that from a bark,' said Harriet.

'*Oont*,' said the hare.

'*Oont?*' said Harriet. 'What does that mean?'

'It's a Leporine word,' said Wiz. 'A sort of mild protest. In this case it means, "Surely, Harriet, you don't think I'd lie to you?"'

'Actually, I don't,' said Harriet. 'I believe everything you tell me, Wiz. And by the way, I've got something to tell *you*. Dad's going to combine the wheat today.'

'In that case I must remember to make myself scarce,' said the hare, 'but before that I'd better make myself into something else. Let's see – how about *Carduelis carduelis*?'

'What's that?'

'Have a look in your bird book.'

Harriet took down from her

shelves *A Field Guide to the Birds of Britain and Europe*, and looked in the index.

'I've found it!' she cried after a bit. 'It's a goldfinch!'

'*Switt-witt-witt-witt!*' piped a voice in reply, and there, perched upon her bedrail, was a beautiful little bird with a head of scarlet, black and white, and black and yellow wings, as colourful as the sparrow had been drab. For a few seconds it fluttered before Harriet's face as though bidding her goodbye, and then it flew out of the window and away.

Watching, Harriet saw the goldfinch alight among a large

patch of thistles in the home paddock and disappear amongst them. A little later, if she had not turned away to get dressed, she would have seen a hare come out of the thistle clump and lope off down the trackway.

After breakfast, when her father had gone out to clean the parlour and yards, Harriet was washing up when Mrs Wisker arrived. Always she made the same remark.

'Puffed I am,' she said, 'pushin' that old bike up the hill. But then, 'tis lovely freewheelin' down again.'

'We're going to cut the wheat on the Ten Acre today, Mrs Wisker,' Harriet said.

'Are you now, my duck? You goin' to ride on the combine?'

'I expect so. To start with anyway.'

'Rabbit-pie then, eh?' said Mrs Wisker.

'I wish he wouldn't shoot them really,' said Harriet. 'I think I might be a vegetarian when I grow up.'

'Bad for you that is,' said Mrs Wisker, 'doin' without meat. I likes my meat. A nice fat rabbit. Or a hare. Now a hare's lovely, my late lamented hubby always said, provided you let it get a bit ripe.'

Harriet shuddered.

'Some people say that hares are witches,' she said.

'Course they are, duck, everybody knows that,' said Mrs Wisker, 'but that don't stop me eating one if I gets half a chance.'

'But you believe in magic, do you, Mrs Wisker?'

'Course I do. Anyone with any sense does, stands to reason. Even my late lamented hubby did and he hadn't no more sense than an old sheep. How else are you goin' to account for that old circle in your dad's wheat? Got to be somethin' funny about that.'

'You don't think it's due to natural causes?'

Mrs Wisker gave a loud piercing shriek, the sort of noise someone makes while being murdered, but Harriet knew it was only her way of laughing.

'Natural causes, duck?' she cried. 'Not on your nelly! 'Tis spaceships as makes 'em, I reckons. UFOs, some do call 'em, but I calls 'em UHTs.'

'UHTs?'

'Unnatural Heavenly Things!'

said Mrs Wisker with another ear-
splitting screech.

Later that morning, once the dew
was off, combining began on the
Ten Acre. A neighbouring farmer
came with his tractor and trailer to
help haul the grain away, while
Harriet's father drove the combine

harvester and she stood beside him on the platform.

At first she could see one or two rabbits moving about in the shelter of the corn, but she knew that it was not until the still uncut square of wheat became quite small that they would begin to break from cover and make a run for it across the stubble.

'I don't want to see you shoot them, Dad!' she shouted above the roar of the machine. 'I don't like it. Let me get down and go home.'

Thank goodness I remembered to warn Wiz, she thought as she walked up the hill, hearing behind her an occasional bang. Though of course if he *had* been in the wheat, he could always have changed himself into something else – a mole perhaps, that would burrow down into the ground out of harm's way.

All the same, after the combining was finished, she had to nerve herself to ask her father if he had shot anything.

'Couple of bunnies,' he said.

'Was that all?'

'And a hare.'

Despite herself, Harriet felt a cold shiver of fear.

'Was it a buck or a doe?' she said. Say it was a doe, please, she thought.

'It was a buck. A big jack-hare. Though I don't see what odds it makes. Either way it'll taste the same.'

Harriet made herself go and look at the three bodies hanging, heads down, in the scullery – two grey, one tawny. By the side of the rabbits, the dead hare looked very long. Its ears hung limply down and there was dried blood on its nose.

It can't be Wiz, she thought.

It *can't*.

Can it?

Chapter Four

'I'm not eating it,' said Harriet at
breakfast next morning.

Her father looked up to see her
spooning cornflakes into her
mouth.

'Not eating what?' he said.

'That hare you shot.'

'Why not?'

'I like hares.'

'Well, you like cornflakes but
you eat enough of them.'

52

'No, I don't mean "like" like that, Daddy. Anyway, I'm not going to eat it.'

'What about the rabbits?'

'Nor them.'

'I was going to give them to Mrs Wisker anyway,' her father said.

'Well, give her the hare too. Please, Dad,' said Harriet.

'Hasn't it struck you,' said her father, 'that I might be looking forward to eating that hare? I'm very fond of jugged hare.'

'Please give it away,' said Harriet in a rather choky voice.

She's near to tears, her father thought. Why? A woman would know, I suppose. It's not easy, trying to be father *and* mother to her.

'OK, Hattie love,' he said. 'Your Wiz can have the lot.'

'What?'

'That's what you call Mrs Wisker, you told me.'

'Oh. Oh yes. Thanks, Dad.'

So the next time Mrs Wisker came to Longhanger Farm, she freewheeled away down the hill again even more happily than usual. In the saddlebag of the ancient bicycle that somehow bore her weight was a hare, and a rabbit swung from each handlebar. As for Harriet, walking about the farm or riding around on Breeze, she looked with mounting impatience for her friend from Pars, so anxious had she now become to prove that he was not in Mrs Wisker's stewpot. Even if he wasn't, he might, she told herself, have assumed some other shape as a change from being a hare. But all the animals she approached ran or hopped or flew away from her.

Until at last, a few days later, she went into the kitchen garden to get some carrots and there was a hare, helping itself to their feathery tops.

Harriet looked hastily around to make sure that neither her father nor Bran were near.

'Wiz?' she said.

'Oh, hello, Harriet,' said the hare with his mouth full. 'Hope you don't mind – these carrot tops are delicious.'

'Where have you been?' said Harriet. 'I've been so worried.'

'Oh, here and there,' said the hare. 'What's been worrying you?'

'Dad shot a hare in the Ten Acre,' said Harriet. 'A buck. I just thought it might be you.'

'*Oont*,' said Wiz.

'What d'you mean?'

'Did you think I was that stupid? You warned me, remember? I spent that day up on the downs – with a friend.'

'I should have known it wasn't you,' said Harriet, and she bent and stroked the hare's yellowy-brown back.

At that instant Bran barked, to say – the hare could have told her – 'Here she is, I've found her,' and Harriet turned to see her father following the dog into the kitchen garden.

'Look out, Wiz!' hissed Harriet from the corner of her mouth, but when she glanced round, he was nowhere to be seen.

'Going to pull some carrots?' her father said.

'Yes.'

'Something's been eating the tops, I see.'

'Yes.'

'Rabbits, I expect.'

'I expect so.'

'I'm going down to the village. Want to come?'

'OK.'

'In about five minutes then,' her father said, and walked off again.

On the stalk of one of the chewed-off carrot tops, Harriet saw, was a snail. For a moment she wondered where on earth Wiz could have got to, and then the penny dropped.

'I should have known it was you,' said Harriet, and she bent and stroked the snail's yellowy-brown back.

Hardly had she left the garden than there sounded a harsh cackling

cry, the alarm call of a startled
blackbird. It was the first and last
blackbird in the world ever to peck
at a small defenceless snail and then,
suddenly and magically, to be
confronted with a large and angry
hare.

That afternoon, Harriet rode up to
the top of the farm and out on to
the open downland, where she let
Breeze have her head. Then she saw
ahead of her not one but two hares,
and she reined the pony in to watch
their curious antics.

They were standing up on their
hind legs and sparring with one
another, striking out with their
forefeet like boxers.

When at last they saw her, their
reactions were opposite. One, the
slightly larger of the two, took to

its heels and raced away until it disappeared from sight. The other came hopping towards her and said, 'Hello!'

'Hello, Wiz,' said Harriet. 'Are you hurt?'

'Hurt?' said the hare.

'Well, you were fighting with that other hare and he was bigger than you.'

'I wasn't fighting,' said Wiz, 'and it wasn't a he.'

'Oh, I'm sorry,' said Harriet. 'I didn't mean to interrupt.'

'That's all right,' said Wiz. 'That's the nice thing about being on holiday – there's no hurry about anything.'

'How much longer are you staying?' said Harriet.

A lot longer, I hope, she thought.

Things will never be the same without my magic hare.

'Well,' said the hare, 'return flights from Earth to Pars are always at the full moon. But don't let's talk about the end of my holidays – I just want to enjoy them. Come on, I'll race you.'

The downs were empty of people that July afternoon, but the hundreds of sheep grazing there stared wide-eyed at the sight of a girl on a strawberry-roan pony galloping flat out over the close-nibbled turf, yet never quite catching a hare that sped effortlessly before them.

At home that evening, Harriet looked in the big diary that her father kept beside the telephone.

Against July 24th, the first day of her own holidays, she had put a tiny 'w'. If her father had noticed it, he would have taken it for a scribble, but it stood for 'Wiz', marking the day she'd met him. Today was the last day of July.

She turned over the double page and there, to her dismay, it said:

Monday, August 2nd
Bank Holiday (Scotland)
Holiday (Republic of Ireland)
O (Full Moon)

'Oh no!' Harriet said. 'Is he only here for two more days?' She turned the pages. The next full moon was on September 1st. On which date would Wiz leave?

All through Sunday she looked about for the hare to ask him, but by the evening of the Monday, the day when the moon was to be at the full, she still had not, as far as she knew, set eyes upon him in any shape or form.

She woke in the middle of that night and went to the window to look out at the great pale disc sailing across the sky with, it seemed to her, the shape of a hare upon it.

Tomorrow, would he be on the way to Pars or still on Longhanger Farm?

The Tuesday was one of Mrs Wisker's days, and when she had arrived and mopped her large red face, and had said what she always said, she added a bit extra.

'What d'you think, duck?' she said to Harriet. 'When I was comin'

up the trackway just now, I looked
out in the paddock and I could see a
shape there, down in the grass.
Well, I remembered what my late
lamented hubby always used to say.
"If you sees a shape in the grass,"

he said, "and when you walks towards it, it gets lower and lower, then 'tis an old hare. If it gets higher and higher as you walks towards it, then 'tis only a lump of muck." Well, I leans the old bike against the fence and I climbs over and I walks towards this shape, and the nearer I gets, the lower it gets. And sure enough it was an old hare. But here's the funny thing, my duck. 'Stead of runnin' off, that hare sits up as bold as brass and looks me in the eye. "Get along with you," I says, and then – would you believe it – he says somethin' back.'

'What!' cried Harriet in disbelief. Surely Wiz hadn't actually spoken to Mrs Wisker!

'What did he say?' she asked.

'Well,' said Mrs Wisker, ' 'twasn't

a proper word, of course. Fancy a hare speakin' English!' and she let out one of her deafening screeches.

'But what was it the hare said?' asked Harriet.

'Sounded like "*oont*",' said Mrs Wisker. 'Hey, where are you goin', duck?' but Harriet was already out of the door.

Down the trackway she ran, pell-mell, and there, calmly cropping the grass of the paddock, was her hare.

'Oh, Wiz!' she cried. 'They didn't come for you then! You're here for another whole month!'

'Certainly,' said the hare. 'Amongst other things, I promised to do you a good turn one of these days, remember? I need a bit of time yet to organize it.'

'Organize what?' asked Harriet.

'A nice surprise, Harriet.'

'What? Tell me! Please!'

'No, no,' said Wiz. 'That might spoil things. You'll just have to wait and see.'

Chapter Five

A little lane ran through the bed of the valley – a lane that led to nowhere except Longhanger Farm – and Harriet now heard a car coming along it and changing down for the sharp turn into the farm trackway.

At the sound of it, Wiz loped off and Harriet climbed back over the fence. The car stopped by her, and a woman put her head out of the window and said, 'Excuse me, but do you have any hens?'

'Yes,' Harriet said.

'I wonder if you could sell me a dozen eggs?'

'Well, we just keep them for ourselves,' said Harriet, 'but I expect I can find you a dozen. They're laying quite well at the moment.'

'That's very kind of you,' said the woman, smiling. 'What's your name, by the way?'

'Harriet Butler.'

'OK, Harriet, you run ahead and I'll meet you up at the farm.'

'Who was that, Mrs Wisker?' said Harriet when the woman had paid for the tray of eggs and driven away again.

'New,' said Mrs Wisker. 'Bought the old turnpike cottage, t'other side of the village. Married woman, she is.'

'How d'you know?'

'Got a big old gold weddin' ring on, hadn't she?'

'I didn't notice,' Harriet said.

'I did!' said Mrs Wisker with a shriek. 'There's not much I don't notice, my late lamented hubby used to say. And I'll tell you another thing I knows about her too.'

'What?'

'She likes an egg for her breakfast,' said Mrs Wisker, screaming yet more loudly.

'Here's one pound fifty, Dad,' Harriet said when her father came in at lunchtime.

'What for?'

'Eggs. I sold a dozen to a lady who came. They've bought the old turnpike cottage, Mrs Wisker said.'

'Perhaps we should get a few more birds,' said her father, 'and then you could earn yourself a bit of pocket money, selling eggs.'

'But you pay for all the food.'

'But you do all the work. Here, have this money back for a start.'

'Look what I've got!' said Harriet to her hare when she met him as she rode on the downs that afternoon.

'Money!' said Wiz. 'The root of all evil.'

'Well, everybody needs some,' Harriet said.

'Hares don't.'

'But you must have money on Pars?'

'Oh yes. But we treat it sensibly. Here on Earth some human beings have so much money they don't know what to do with it, and some are desperately poor. On Pars everyone's equal. Much fairer.'

'Are you looking forward to going back?' Harriet asked.

'It'll be nice to see my friends again,' said the hare.

'Have you got lots?'

'We're all friends on Pars. There's no such word as "enemy" in the language.'

'I'm your friend, aren't I, Wiz?'

'Certainly,' said the hare, and Breeze whinnied loudly.

'What's she saying?' asked Harriet.

'She's saying, "Why are we standing here while you chatter away to that old hare, when we could be having a good gallop?" Come on – race you!'

'You always win,' said Harriet. 'You're faster than Breeze.'

'All right,' said Wiz, 'we'll make it a handicap. Go on, off you go.'

Any minute now he'll pass me,
Harriet thought as she urged the
pony on, but no hare appeared
beside her. When at last she drew
rein, she looked round but there
was no sign of Wiz. She rode back,
puzzled, and after a while she came
upon a hedgehog waddling along.

'Whatever are you doing up here
on the downs?' she said, and the
hedgehog gave a kind of grunt.

Harriet rode a little further,
looking for Wiz, but then she heard
a voice behind her.

'You won,' said the voice and,
wheeling the pony round, Harriet
saw not a hedgehog but a hare.

'It was you!' she said, laughing.
'A sparrow, a goldfinch, a snail and
now a hedgehog. Whatever will
you turn into next, I wonder?'

'A Partian, next full moon,' said
the hare.

'I shall miss you,' said Harriet. 'I
told Dad I wasn't lonely here on the
farm, but I shall be when you've
gone and it's just the two of us
again.'

'*Oont*,' said the hare.

'Why, what have I said wrong?'

'You'll see, before long, sure as eggs is eggs.'

'That's what I got that money for,' said Harriet. 'I sold some eggs to a lady who came to the farm. Dad says we can get some more hens, and then I can sell lots.'

'Perhaps she'll come back for more, this lady,' said Wiz.

'She might.'

'She will.'

'How do you know?'

'Hares are witches, aren't they?'

By the time the newcomer to the village came again to Longhanger Farm, Mrs Wisker had found out a lot more about her.

'She's a book-writer,' she told Harriet. 'Writes little books for kiddies, they say, though she's got no children of her own. Mrs Lambert, she's called, but there ain't no sign of Mr Lambert yet. I expect she's gettin' the old place straight first. Any road, she seems to like your eggs, my duck. Goin' to come regular, she said, didn't she?'

'Yes,' said Harriet. 'She's my first customer.'

The next time that Mrs Lambert came to the farm to buy eggs was not on one of Mrs Wisker's days.

'All alone, Harriet?' she said when the door was opened.

'Yes. Dad's ploughing the Ten Acre.'

'I think I must have seen him as I came along the lane. I saw a green tractor. Can I have some more of your big brown eggs, please, Harriet? By the way, I should have said – my name is Lambert, Jessica Lambert.'

'You write stories for children, don't you?' asked Harriet as she filled a tray with eggs.

'Yes, for very young children.'

'What about?'

'Animals, mostly. Possibly your mother read you one or two of my books when you were little?'

'I wouldn't know,' Harriet said. 'She died when I was very small.'

'Oh. Sorry. I didn't know.'

'That's all right,' said Harriet.

Little did she think, as she watched her customer drive away, that she would see her again so soon. For not ten minutes later the door–bell rang again, and there on the step stood Mrs Lambert, a bloodstained handkerchief held to her nose.

'Whatever's happened?' cried Harriet.

'I've had a bit of an accident,' Mrs Lambert said. 'I had to swerve suddenly in the lane, and the car went into the ditch and I banged my face. It's nothing much, just a nosebleed I think, that's all, but the car's stuck and I wondered – d'you think your father would come and pull me out with his tractor?'

'Yes,' said Harriet, 'of course he would. I'll go and fetch him. D'you want to wash your face? Would you like a clean hanky?'

'Yes please, Harriet,' said Mrs Lambert. 'Then I'll go back down to the car and wait for help.'

A little later, Harriet's father got down from the cab of the big green tractor and held out a hand.

'John Butler,' he said. 'How do you do?'

'Not very well, I'm afraid,' said Mrs Lambert.

'You haven't broken your nose?'

'No, I don't think so. And I hope there's nothing broken in the car. It's just that I can't get out of the ditch because the nearside wheels are spinning.'

'We'll soon have you out of there,' said Harriet's father, busy with a rope, and sure enough the big tractor pulled the little car out as easy as winking.

'All's well that ends well,' said Harriet's father as he unhitched the tow rope.

'Not quite,' said Harriet. 'There *is* something broken — in the back of the car.'

'What?' said Mrs Lambert.

'Every single egg you just bought,' said Harriet.

Mrs Lambert smiled ruefully.

'All the fault of that silly animal,' she said. 'I had to swerve to avoid running over it. It suddenly came out of the hedge and calmly sat up in the middle of the lane as though all it wanted was for me to go in the ditch.'

'This animal,' said Harriet's father. 'What was it?'

'A hare.'

Chapter Six

Was it Wiz? Harriet thought.

Whatever was he playing at, sitting in the middle of the lane? He could easily have been run over and then he'd never have seen Pars again.

Was it a hare? her father thought.

These people who came from the town to live in the country couldn't tell a hare from a rabbit. Probably it was an old tomcat, anyway.

'You're sure it was a hare?' he said.

He thinks I'm a townie who can't tell a hare from a rabbit, Mrs Lambert thought.

'I know a *Lepus europaeus occidentalis* when I see one,' she said.

'I don't follow you.'

'It's Latin for the Brown Hare, Dad,' said Harriet.

'However do you know that?'

'I learned it,' said Harriet truthfully.

'From a book, I expect,' said Jessica Lambert. 'Like me. I illustrate my own little stories, you see, so I have to be careful that I know what a particular animal looks like. I don't want to make silly mistakes and end up with egg on my face.'

'Talking of which,' said Harriet's

father, 'you must let us give you some more eggs in place of the broken ones. And, more importantly, how is your face?'

'My nose is a bit sore.'

'And I'm afraid you're going to have a shiner,' Harriet's father said.

'What's a shiner, Dad?' asked Harriet.

'A black eye. Look here, Mrs Lambert, you must be a bit shaken. Why don't you turn round and come on back up to the farm, and we'll find you some more eggs and give you a cup of tea?'

Anyone watching would have seen quite a procession going back up the trackway to Longhanger Farm.

The little car led the way, the big tractor followed, and close behind it trotted the sheepdog, Bran. A

hundred metres or so behind Bran,
a hare came loping up the hill.

Just as he reached the yard, some
instinct made the dog turn his head
to look back, but all he saw was an
old crow hopping about, that cried,
'*Caark!*' at him.

'Do please sit down, Mrs
Lambert,' said the farmer. 'And put
the kettle on, please, Hat.'

'Isn't it awful,' said Mrs
Lambert, 'the way we all get our
names shortened?'

'You can't shorten mine much,'
said John Butler.

'No! But what I mean is, for
example – my name is Jessica (and

please stop calling me Mrs
Lambert), which is quite a nice
name, I think, as is Harriet. But my
husband always called me Jess,
which sounds like a sheepdog.'

'It sounds nice enough to me,'
said Harriet's father.

'I'd rather you called me Jessica.'

'If you call me John.'

'It's a deal.'

'What's a deal?' asked Harriet, coming back from the kitchen. 'I hope you're not making Mrs Lambert pay for some more eggs, Daddy. It's my fault the first lot got broken.'

'Your fault?' said Mrs Lambert.

'Well, yes, in a way. It was my hare that caused the accident.'

'Your hare?' said her father.

'Well . . . I mean . . . our hare. A Longhanger Farm hare.'

'A crazy hare,' said her father. 'There must be a story there for you, Jessica – *The Mad Hare of Longhanger Farm*.'

As Mrs Lambert drove away again, with half a dozen fresh eggs for which Harriet would take no payment, she suddenly saw a hare (*the* hare? she thought) squatting by the side of the trackway. She slowed down to an absolute crawl, watching it like a hawk, and out of the window she said, 'You're not going to do anything silly, are you?'

To her surprise, the animal made a soft but distinct noise in reply. It sounded like '*Oont.*'

'She's nice, isn't she, Dad?' Harriet was saying.

'Very,' said her father.

Why, he thought, did she say, 'My husband *called* me Jess?'

'I suppose Mr Lambert will turn up before long,' he said in an offhand way. 'I imagine she's getting the old cottage straight first.'

'That's what Mrs Wisker said.'

'There's not much she doesn't notice.'

'As her late lamented hubby used to say,' said Harriet, and they both laughed.

When Mrs Wisker arrived next day, Harriet told her the whole story of the accident.

'Poor soul!' said Mrs Wisker. 'And got a black eye too! Not the first she'd've had, from what I hear.'

'What do you mean?' asked Harriet.

'That husband of hers. Free with his fists, they say, specially when he'd had a drop too much, which was often.'

'How horrible!' said Harriet.

'He won't do it no more, duck. She got rid of him, for good and all.'

'Murdered him, d'you mean?'

Mrs Wisker gave one of her loudest shrieks.

'You been seein' too much telly,' she said. 'No – dee-vorced him. Couple of year ago.'

Last thing that day, Harriet was leaning out of her bedroom window, scanning the valley below as usual.

The evening sunshine lay warmly on the fields, and on the cows and sheep that grazed them or lay and chewed their cud, and turned to a purplish colour the furrows of the newly ploughed Ten Acre, where once, not long ago, she had first seen the corn circle.

A few rabbits hopped about the headlands of the pastures but there was no sign of a hare.

So still did Harriet keep that a sparrow alighted on the windowsill, but when she said, 'Wiz?' it flew hastily away again.

Her father came in to say good-night.

'Dad,' she said. 'You know Mrs Lambert.'

'Yes.'

'Well, Mrs Wisker says she's divorced.'

'Oh, really?'

'Yes. Dad, can I ask you something?'

'Yes.'

'When are we going to get some more hens?'

Chapter Seven

For a few days, Harriet saw no sign of her hare.

She had plenty to occupy her anyway, because, rather to her surprise, her father had lost no time in buying her a dozen pullets at the point of lay.

So Harriet was busy admiring them and accustoming them to the rest of the flock and enjoying the

excitement of collecting their very
first, rather small, eggs. In
addition, she had made a signboard
and painted on it in large letters:

FRESH FREE–RANGE
FARM EGGS FOR SALE
HARRIET BUTLER
LONGHANGER FARM

She put the notice up at the end
of the lane where it joined the road,

and afterwards she walked down there several times, just to admire it.

Coming back one morning, she looked over a gate at the herd, which was grazing a laneside field, and saw that there was one beast standing all by itself in a far corner, a long way from the others. Harriet was not a farmer's daughter for nothing. She knew that if a cow isolates itself in this way, it very often means either that it is going to give birth or that it is ill. She walked across to have a look at it.

Harriet knew all the herd by name – Bluebell the master cow and her special crony Buttercup, and Dahlia and Rose and Pansy and all the rest. Each had different markings that she knew, but she did not recognize this solitary cow.

Was it a neighbour's that had somehow got in with the Longhanger herd? Was it a new one that her father had recently bought? She could not see any numbered sale ticket stuck on its rump.

'Who are you?' she said as she reached it. 'And what's the matter? You seem healthy enough, and you certainly don't look as if you're going to calve. Why aren't you grazing with the rest? Off your food, are you?'

Since the cow made no reply to any of these questions, Harriet looked about for something to tempt it with. She saw a nice patch of white clover and bent to pull a bunch of it.

'Try this, old girl,' she said, straightening up again to see not a cow, but the hare.

'Less of the "old girl", Harriet,'
said Wiz.

'Oh!' cried Harriet. 'Why ever
did you want to turn yourself into a
cow?'

'Just to see if I liked it.'

'And did you?'

'Not a lot. I've tried being quite a
few different animals since we last
met, but there's nothing to touch a
hare.'

'Something jolly nearly *did* touch a hare the other day,' said Harriet. 'Whatever were you doing sitting in the middle of the lane like that? It *was* you, wasn't it?'

'Certainly.'

'Well, to begin with, you could have been killed.'

'To end with, you mean. But I wasn't.'

'And Mrs Lambert might have been badly hurt.'

'But she wasn't.'

'Whatever were you playing at, Wiz?'

'Judge not the play before the play be done,' said the hare.

'I don't understand.'

'You will. Trust me, Harriet. I know what is best for you.'

Harriet sat down on the ground and chewed a piece of grass and watched the hare eating the clover.

'Before long, my holidays will be halfway through,' she said.

'Mine too,' said the hare. 'The waxing moon will before long be full, and then I shall go.'

'I don't want you to,' Harriet said. 'I shall be very unhappy never to see you again.'

'On the contrary,' said Wiz, 'you are going to be very happy. And though you may perhaps not see me again, you will always be reminded of me throughout your life, perhaps as many as a thousand times, if you live to be a very old woman.'

'How?'

'By looking at each full moon. You will always see upon it the shape of a hare.'

'Because of you,' Harriet said,

'they will always be my favourite animals.'

'Ah, Harriet!' said Wiz. 'You will always be my favourite human being.'

At this point they heard a car coming along the lane towards the farm.

'I must go, Wiz,' Harriet said. 'It might be someone wanting eggs.'

'Or someone bringing you a present?' said the hare.

It's not my birthday, thought Harriet as she ran back across the field, so why should anyone be bringing me a present? And how could Wiz possibly know, anyway?

By the time she reached the bottom of the farm trackway, the car was coming back down again, and she could see that it was Mrs Lambert's.

'Did you want eggs?' Harriet asked.

'No, not yet,' said Jessica Lambert, 'though I saw your posh new notice. No, I came to see you, but your Mrs Wisker said you'd gone out somewhere. She seemed very interested in what's left of my black eye. You must have told her all about it.'

'Yes. I'm glad it's better. What did you want to see me for?'

'To give you a present.'

That Wiz, thought Harriet – he's magic.

'It's for both of you really,' said Jessica Lambert. 'For you and your father. Just to say thank you for rescuing me the other day,' and she handed a small flat parcel out of the car window. 'Good luck with the egg business, Harriet!' she said, and drove off.

'That Mrs Lambert's been,' said Mrs Wisker when Harriet came into the farmhouse. 'Lookin' for you, she was.'

'I met her,' Harriet said.

Mrs Wisker looked at the parcel.

'Present?' she said.

'Yes.'

'Not your birthday, is it, duck?'

'No.'

'Somethin' for your dad, is it?'

'I expect so,' Harriet said.

Mrs Wisker let out a loud screech.

'What you mean is, "Mind your own business and get on with your cleanin', Mrs Wisker," and that's what I'd better be doin'. Too nosy by half I am, my late lamented hubby used to say.'

Harriet longed to be nosy too, to open the parcel and see what was in it. But it's for Dad as well, she said to herself, and she waited until Mrs Wisker had freewheeled off and her father had come in for his lunch.

'Mrs Lambert came again this morning,' she said.

'More eggs?'

'No. This.'

'What is it?'

'A present for us, she said. Open it, Dad.'

'You open it, Hat.'

Carefully, Harriet undid the paper wrapping.

'It feels like a framed picture,' she said, and then, 'Oh look, Dad!'

It was a beautifully detailed little portrait of a hare. The artist had caught precisely the slightly shorter head and redder shoulders of the jack-hare, and there was a look of high intelligence in the prominent brown eye.

In the bottom right-hand corner were two tiny initials, J.L., and opposite, in very small print, the creature's Latin name.

'How lovely,' said Harriet's father. 'But why should she take so much trouble?'

'Because we helped her when she had her accident,' said Harriet.

'Look, she's even put *Lepus europaeus ACCIDENTALIS*!'

'It's wonderfully lifelike,' said her father. 'Somehow it's not just any old hare, it's a very special one.'

'Yes,' said Harriet. 'It is.'

Chapter Eight

Harriet was cantering Breeze across a stretch of downland when she saw a hare behaving in an odd way.

It was leaping round and round in a circle, kicking up its heels. As she drew near, the hare stopped this strange behaviour and sat awaiting her, so she knew it must be Wiz.

'Whatever were you doing?' she said.

'Just skipping about,' said Wiz.

'Why?'

'*Joie de vivre.*'

'Is that French?'

'*Oui.*'

'What does it mean?'

'The joy of living. I'm just glad to be alive.'

I'm glad I shan't see you dead, standing upright in a bottle, thought Harriet. You wouldn't look like a hare, of course, you'd look like a Partian, and I'm quite glad I don't know what Partians look like.

'But you're not going to die for ages, are you, Wiz?' she said.

'Hope not,' said the hare. 'I want to cram in a lot more happy holidays before I'm bottled.'

'To Earth?'

'Perhaps.'

'To Longhanger Farm?'

'Who knows? If I don't return for some time, you won't be here any more. You'll be living somewhere else, married probably, with a pack of kids.'

'Have you got any children, Wiz?'

'On Pars, you mean?'

'Yes.'

'No.'

'Well, you couldn't possibly have any children on Earth, could you now?' said Harriet, but the hare did not reply.

Harriet sighed.

'It's a funny thing about holidays,' she said, 'but once you get about halfway through them, the rest of the time simply flies. Before you know it, I'll be back at school and you'll have gone. The

next full moon is on September the
first. That's less than a couple of
weeks away now.'

'Time for lots of surprises,' said
Wiz.

As usual he was right.

To begin with, on the very next
day Harriet had three new egg
customers.

'We can't have anything eggy to
eat today, Dad,' she said to her
father. 'I've sold them all.'

'The pullets' eggs as well?'

'Yes. I charged much less for
them, of course, because they're
still rather small.'

'Quite the business woman.'

'Yes, but I'm worried about my
first customer. Suppose she wants
some?'

'Jessica Lambert, d'you mean?'

Harriet nodded.

'Well, she'll just have to buy some from the village shop. I'll tell her. I'm going down there this evening.'

'What for?'

'To thank her for the picture of the hare, of course. You coming?'

'Callin' on Mrs Lambert, were you, duck?' said Mrs Wisker next morning.

'How did you know?' said Harriet.

Mrs Wisker gave one of her screams.

'She don't drive a Land Rover,' she said, 'and there was one parked outside the old turnpike cottage yesterday evenin'. Any road, I seen you comin' out. Hour and twenty-three minutes you was there. Nice, was it?'

'Yes,' said Harriet. 'She showed me all the books she's written. She does the pictures too, you know.'

'Like that one of a hare you got in the sittin'-room?'

'You don't miss much, Mrs Wisker, do you?' said Harriet.

'Only my late lamented hubby!' said Mrs Wisker with another screech.

One thing you don't know, thought Harriet, is that Dad's asked Mrs Lambert to supper this coming Saturday. And he's going to cook Seven-hour Lamb, and I'm going to make a fresh-fruit salad, and I'm going to be allowed to stay up really late.

The weather was perfect that Saturday evening, August 21st. They sat out in the warmth of the old walled garden at the back of the farmhouse, and Mrs Lambert and Harriet's father drank wine, and Harriet drank Coke, and Bran ate Twiglets in the sunshine.

Almost the first thing that happened was that Mrs Lambert said to Harriet (in the nicest way, with the nicest smile), 'Harriet, you are to stop calling me Mrs Lambert, d'you understand?'

'Yes, Jessica,' said Harriet, and they all laughed, comfortably. And the Seven-hour Lamb, with lots of vegetables from the garden, was beautifully tender, and the fresh-fruit salad, with lots of cream, was perfectly delicious, and everybody happily ate too much.

'Time you went to bed, Hat,' said John Butler at last.

'But Dad,' said Harriet, 'you

promised I could stay up really late.'

'You already have,' said her father. 'It's gone eleven o'clock.'

In bed, Harriet lay and thought how strange it was to hear the murmur of voices in the room below, and how nice it was to think that Dad had someone to talk to.

A little later, she heard the voices outside, below her open window.

'Thank you so much, John, it's been a perfect evening,' said one voice.

'Thank you for coming, Jessica,' said the other voice.

Then, after a little pause, Harriet heard a car door shut and an engine start. The noise of it fell away as the car went down the hill, and Harriet fell asleep.

When she woke next morning, there was the hare, sitting beside the bed.

'How did you get here?' she said.

'Sparrow again,' said Wiz. 'I couldn't be bothered with anything fancy. Just called to see how your supper party went.'

'How did you know?' Harriet said. 'You're worse than Mrs Wisker.'

'I know lots of things that you don't know I know,' said Wiz. 'Like what's going to happen next Thursday, for example.'

'What *is* going to happen?'

'A surprise. I told you there'd be surprises.'

Harriet looked at the calendar hanging on the wall by her bed.

'Next Thursday's the twenty-sixth,' she said, but she found she

was talking to a sparrow that cheeped at her and flew out of the window.

Later that morning the phone rang.

'Longhanger Farm,' said Harriet.

'Oh Harriet, it's Jessica. Is your father there?'

'No, he's out in the yard somewhere.'

'Doesn't matter, you can ask him later. The thing is, I've got to go up to London to see my publishers this week, and I wondered if you'd like to come with me? We could go and see some of the sights and generally have a day out, if you'd like to.'

'I'd love to, Jessica!' said Harriet. 'I'll ask Dad if I can. What day?'

'Thursday. That's the twenty-sixth.'

'D'you want to go?' Harriet's father said when she asked him.

'Oh yes, please!'

'You like Jessica, don't you?'

'Of course. Don't you?'

John Butler smiled.

'You give her a ring,' he said, 'and tell her it's OK by me. I'm sure you'll have a lovely day.'

And they did.

On the twenty-sixth, Jessica collected Harriet really early in the morning. They drove to the station and got on the train, something Harriet had hardly ever done before. Then, when they reached London, Harriet was taken into the publishers' offices where they made a fuss of her. And then they saw the Changing of the Guard at Buckingham Palace, and had a lovely lunch, and went to Madame Tussauds, and, last of all, to the Planetarium where Harriet looked in vain for the planet Pars.

It's too far away, she said to herself. They haven't discovered it yet. I'm the only person who knows about it.

By the time they arrived back at Longhanger Farm, the afternoon milking was finished and the herd was coming down the trackway, Bluebell at the head, Bran and his master behind.

They waited until the cows had gone past and then they got out of the car and crossed the lane to join the farmer and lean on the gate, watching the big black-and-white animals fanning out across the sunlit meadow.

'Good day, Hat?' asked Harriet's father.

'It was smashing, Daddy,' said Harriet, and she told him all the things they'd done.

'How about you, Jessica?' said John Butler. 'How were things at your publishers?'

'Well, they seem to like my latest story.'

'What's it about, Jessica?' asked Harriet.

'A hare. Doing that little picture for you gave me some ideas.'

'Talk of the devil!' said the farmer, and he pointed out into the field.

There, they saw, was a hare, leaping round and round in a circle, kicking up its heels.

'I wonder why it's behaving like that,' said Jessica.

'I don't know,' said John.

'I do,' said Harriet. 'It's *joie de vivre*.'

Chapter Nine

It was the final weekend of Harriet's summer holidays.

'And of Wiz's too,' she said to Breeze as she was mucking out the loose-box, watched by Bran.

The pony blew through her nostrils and the dog whined softly, as though they knew how Harriet was feeling.

'Life's never going to be quite the

same again without my hare,' she said. 'No more magic, no more surprises. He promised to do me a good turn one of these days. I suppose that must have been the trip to London with Jessica. And talk about trips – just think how far he'll be going on Wednesday night when the moon is full. When I was in the Planetarium, I looked to see which was the furthest away and it was Pluto, but Pars is probably ten times further. I suppose he'll change into a Partian before he gets into the spacecraft. I wonder where it will land?'

Later, she walked down the trackway and across the first field to the one beyond where, a mere five weeks ago, she had seen that corn circle in the wheat.

Now it had been ploughed and

worked down and sown with a grass-seed mixture, and already there was a faint tinge of green against the brown earth.

There was something else brown there too, she could see, just where the corn circle had been, and because it sank as she walked towards it, she knew it was a hare and not just a lump of muck.

Not until Harriet was almost upon it did the hare spring up and run away, and she bent down and put her hand in the slight hollow of its form, and felt the warmth of it.

'Well, you weren't Wiz,' she said, and a voice behind her said, 'Too true.'

'Oh,' said Harriet to her hare, 'was that a friend of yours?'

'You could say that,' replied Wiz. 'I'm afraid I frightened him.'

'*Oont*,' said the hare, the only word of the Leporine language that Harriet had ever heard. It meant disapproval, she knew.

'What have I said wrong?' she asked.

'You didn't frighten *him*, you frightened *her*,' said Wiz. 'I've tried to tell her that you wouldn't hurt her, but she has no confidence in humans. Let's hope her children may grow to be more trusting.'

'Children? She has babies?'

'Her three leverets are in this field. Unlike their mother, they will not move when you approach, for she has told them to keep perfectly still. Each one has been left in a different part of the field and, when you have gone, she will go to each in turn to feed it.'

'Why aren't they all in a nest

together,' asked Harriet, 'like baby rabbits would be?'

'Baby rabbits,' said Wiz, 'can afford to be born blind and naked and helpless, because they're safe underground. But hares live above ground, so the leverets stand a better chance of survival if they're separated. Come, I will show you.'

So Harriet followed as Wiz led her in turn to each of the three recently born babies. Like all leverets, they had come into the world with a covering of hair, open-eyed and able to run, but they all lay still as stone as Harriet bent and gently stroked them.

'Three little does,' said Wiz.

'They're lovely!' said Harriet.

'Aren't you going to congratulate me then?'

'You mean . . .? Oh Wiz! How

wonderful! To think that when you've gone, your daughters will still be here! Will they be magic?'

'They won't talk to you, or change into other creatures, if that's what you mean. But I like to think that maybe they'll be a little different from the average hare.'

'How shall I know them from other hares, once they're grown?'

'Because, unlike other hares, they will never run away from you. I am going to teach them that right away, now that they've seen you. They will run from any other human being, or from any enemy like a dog or fox. But if, in time to come, you chance upon a hare that remains lying in its form and allows you to stroke it, that will be one of my daughters.'

'That will be brilliant!' said

Harriet. They'll always remind me of you, Wiz, she thought as she walked home. Not that I could ever forget you.

Jessica Lambert came that afternoon for eggs, and Harriet said to her suddenly, 'Do you believe in magic?'

'Of course I do,' said Jessica. 'Anyone with any sense does.'

You sound just like Mrs Wisker, Harriet thought.

'Can animals be magical?' she said.

'Some can,' said Jessica. 'Hares have always been thought to be beasts of magic.'

That's exactly what Wiz said, thought Harriet.

'Dad shot one when he was combining,' she said.

Jessica sighed.

'Oh dear,' she said. 'I wish he wouldn't shoot them, really.'

And now, thought Harriet, you sound like me.

'Couldn't you ask him not to?' she said.

'Why don't you?'

'He'd take more notice of you.'

'Why don't we both ask him?'

So they did.

'What's all this?' John Butler said. 'An anti-bloodsports deputation?'

'No,' said Jessica. 'We're not trying to stop you potting the rabbits and pigeons that damage your crops. We're just asking you not to shoot hares again.'

'Ever,' said Harriet.

'Why not?'

'Because,' said Jessica, 'we both happen to be rather fond of hares.'

'I'm fond of hare too!'

'To eat, he means!' cried Harriet, close to tears. 'Please, Dad, say you won't!'

'All right, all right,' said her father. 'I hereby solemnly promise that I will never again shoot a hare on Longhanger Farm. Will that do?'

'Yes,' they said. 'That will do.'

'And come and have Sunday lunch with me, both of you,' said Jessica. 'I'll do you roast beef and all the trimmings.'

'It seems funny,' said Harriet to her father when her first customer had driven away, 'to be still making Jessica pay for her eggs. I mean, you ought to *give* your friends things, not make them pay.'

'Maybe she won't be buying them for much longer,' Harriet's father said.

'Why not?'

'Oh . . . I don't know . . . she might be moving house.'

'Oh, I hope not!' said Harriet.

And I hope so, said her father, but he said it to himself.

Chapter Ten

'Penny for your thoughts, Harriet,'
said Jessica at the end of Sunday
lunch.

Harriet had been quiet
throughout the meal, leaving the
grown-ups to do the talking.

'She's miles away somewhere,'
her father said.

Soon, thought Harriet, my hare
will be *millions* of miles away. He's

only got three more days of his holidays left.

'Jessica,' she said. 'Does your hare story have a happy ending?'

'Oh yes,' said Jessica. 'I like happy endings.'

'Me too,' said Harriet's father, 'so let me give you a hand with the washing-up and that'll be a happy ending to a lovely lunch.'

'Can I help?' said Harriet.

'Actually,' said her father quickly, 'I was just going to ask you to do something for me, Hattie. Could you go on ahead and just check on old Buttercup? She's due to calve any time now and I forgot to have a look at her as we drove down here. I shan't be long. I'll probably catch you up before you reach home.'

'OK,' said Harriet.

Funny, she thought as she walked through the village and turned into the lane. He could just as easily have looked at Buttercup himself on the way back.

She went into the cow pasture and walked around the herd. Several cows were lying down, comfortably cudding, Buttercup amongst them.

'She doesn't look as though she has any immediate plans for calving,' said a familiar voice, and there was Wiz, hopping towards her.

He knows everything about everything, thought Harriet as she squatted down to stroke her hare.

'I named you well,' she said. 'You're a wizard.'

'And you're a very special girl, Harriet,' said the hare, 'and it's nice

to think that I'm going to do you
that good turn I promised.'

'You mean you haven't done it
yet? I thought it was the London
trip. Or perhaps teaching your
daughters to trust me.'

'No. The really big surprise that I
have arranged for you is actually
beginning to happen at this very
minute, as we speak.'

'I don't understand,' said Harriet.

'You will,' said Wiz, 'when the moon is full.'

'Do you mean that the surprise is that you're not going yet after all? You're going to stay longer?'

'No, I'm going all right. By the time you understand what I'm talking about, I'll be gone.'

'But then I shan't be able to thank you for whatever it is.'

'I don't need thanks, Harriet. It is I who am grateful to you for making my holiday on Earth such fun. All I ask you to do is to be kind to my daughters, to all hares, to all animals, for the rest of your long life.'

'I will, I will!' said Harriet.

She looked earnestly into the hare's large brown eyes.

'Are you telling me that I'm

going to live to be very old?' she asked.

'Certainly,' replied Wiz. 'You will see a thousand full moons in your time.'

Harriet smiled happily.

'Oh, Wiz!' she said. 'I believe every word you say.'

She got to her feet and watched the hare lolloping slowly away across the pasture. Then she shouted after him: 'I suppose you know exactly when old Buttercup here is going to calve?'

'Certainly,' said the hare. 'Tuesday morning. Ten o'clock. Heifer calf,' and off he went.

Harriet was just turning into the trackway when she heard the Land Rover coming along the lane. Her father stopped. What's he looking so pleased about? she thought.

'Buttercup all right?' he asked as she got in.

'Oh yes, she's not doing anything. I should say she'll calve about the middle of Tuesday morning.'

'Indeed?' said her father. 'Perhaps you'd tell me the exact time, Miss Clever Clogs?'

'Ten o'clock. And she'll have a heifer calf.'

John Butler laughed.

'Well, I hope she does,' he said. 'She's a good milker, old Buttercup, but she's always had bull calves. I'd like a daughter of hers.'

Harriet thought of Wiz's children, as the Land Rover rattled up the trackway. He seemed pleased to have daughters.

'When I was born,' she said,

'were you glad I was a girl, Dad?'

'Very glad,' said her father. 'And so was your mother.'

She didn't have a very long life, thought Harriet, but it seems that I'm going to. I suppose Wiz could tell me all sorts of things that are going to happen to me if I asked, but I don't want to know. All I want for now is just to be here on Longhanger Farm with my dad.

She looked at his strong hand on the steering-wheel and put hers on top of it.

'Are you happy, Dad?' she asked.

'Very happy, Hat,' he said. 'Why do you ask? Don't tell me you can predict my future as well as Buttercup's?'

He laughed again.

'A heifer calf at exactly ten

o'clock on Tuesday morning!' he said. 'Pigs might fly!'

The next day – Monday, August 30th – Harriet was clearing up the breakfast things when Mrs Wisker arrived.

'Puffed I am,' she said, 'pushin' that old bike up the hill. But then 'tis lovely freewheelin' down again. I just hope it don't come on to rain. We shall get some sure enough, the cows is all lyin' down and there was a red sky this mornin' and the swallows is all flyin' low. Oh, and I tell you what, duck – I seen that old hare again just now as I was comin' up. Sittin' up bold as brass it was.'

'Did he say anything to you?' said Harriet.

Mrs Wisker gave her usual ear-splitting shriek of laughter.

'Say anything?' she cried. 'Oh you're a scream, you are, duck!'

It's you that's the scream, thought Harriet.

'Is the hare still there?' she asked.

'Far as I know,' said Mrs Wisker. 'You want to tell your dad to get his gun – he gave me a lovely hare, harvest time.'

When Harriet walked down the trackway, she found Wiz feeding quietly beside the fence.

'Did you want me?' she said.

'Yes,' said the hare. 'Just to give you a weather warning. Were you thinking of going riding today?'

'Yes, I was. I thought I'd ride up to the downs this morning and we could have a race. But don't be a hedgehog this time.'

'Don't go,' said the hare, 'unless you want to risk being struck by lightning. There's going to be a humdinger of a thunderstorm in a couple of hours time. Come tomorrow morning instead. I'll look out for you.'

'All right,' said Harriet. 'But not till the afternoon. I want to see Dad's face when Buttercup's calf arrives.'

Even as the hare loped off, Harriet heard a rumble of thunder in the far distance, and by the time Mrs Wisker had finished her cleaning and was ready to go home, the storm was banging and crashing right overhead, with lightning to match.

'I'm not goin' in that,' said Mrs Wisker. 'The old bike might get struck, and then it wouldn't only be

my hubby as was late lamented,
'twould be me too,' and she waited
an extra hour, flicking a duster
about, until the storm had passed.

On the following morning, the last
day of August, Harriet's father
came in for breakfast after the
morning milking and said, 'I'm
beginning to wonder if you're
going to be right.'

'What about, Dad?' asked
Harriet.

'Old Buttercup's thinking about
calving. I left her out in the pasture
when I brought the rest in.'

'I'll meet you down there, ten
o'clock sharp,' said Harriet.

And at ten o'clock sharp, as
father and daughter stood and
watched, Buttercup dropped a fine
heifer calf.

'Dad was really amazed!' shouted Harriet that afternoon, as Breeze galloped across the downland turf, the hare running easily alongside.

'Your turn next!' cried Wiz, and he sprinted ahead, to win the race easily.

'What did you mean?' asked Harriet, when she had slipped off the puffing pony. 'My turn next?'

'To be amazed,' said Wiz, and no

matter how she questioned him, he
would say no more.

'I cannot understand,' said Harriet's
father when he came to say good-
night at the end of the day, 'how
you were so sure about that
calving. How did you know?'

'You wouldn't believe me if I told
you, Dad,' said Harriet, and no
matter how he questioned her, she
would say no more, except that at
last she said, 'Rabbits!'

It was their custom – something
taught to John Butler as a boy and
to his father before him – that on
the last day of each month, the last
word you spoke before going to
sleep was 'Rabbits!' and that when
you woke next morning on the first
of the new month, the first word

you uttered was 'Hares!' To do this
was to ensure good luck.

So Harriet's father duly replied,
'Rabbits!' and kissed her and went
downstairs.

'Hares!' said Harriet loudly, the
moment she woke on Wednesday,
September 1st, and then her
spirits sank like a stone as she
remembered.

Tonight the moon was at the full.
Tonight she was to lose her hare.

Chapter Eleven

Harriet dressed and went to let out
her hens and to feed the calves. As
usual, she looked in through the
door of the milking-parlour and
called, 'Morning, Daddy.'

'Hares!' said her father. 'You're
meant to say, Hares!'

'I already have.'

'Oh, that's all right then.'

No, it's not all right, said Harriet

to herself. It's supposed to bring good luck but how could it when Wiz was going? Would she even set eyes on him again before he went?

All morning she wandered about the farm hoping to see her hare, but there was no sign of him. And when in the afternoon she rode over the downs, calling his name, there was no answer except the bleating of sheep, the sad cries of lapwings, and the sigh of the wind.

But when, in the evening, Harriet went out into the kitchen garden to pick the last of the scarlet runners, she found that someone else had got there first.

'Hope you don't mind,' said the hare, standing on his hind legs to pull down a bean pod, 'but I couldn't resist a last snack.'

'Don't you have vegetables on Pars?' Harriet asked.

'Heavens, no! We live on synthetic, additive-free, low-cholesterol pills,' said Wiz. 'I shall miss being a hare.'

'I shall miss you,' said Harriet, 'dreadfully.'

Wiz bit through the bean pod with his two large front teeth and began to chew, moving his lower jaw from side to side.

'Very suitable for hares, these beans,' he said.

'Why?'

'They're both runners.'

Harriet stood watching, without saying anything.

'It was supposed to be a joke,' said Wiz.

'I'm sorry,' said Harriet. 'I don't feel like laughing.'

'*Oont*,' said the hare. He swallowed his mouthful and looked directly up at her. 'Listen to me, Harriet,' he said. 'You mustn't feel sad. Look at it from my point of view. I'm an alien on a strange planet, and though I've had a lovely time, I'm looking forward to going home, to Pars, to my friends. Of course I shall miss you, but I'm

happy to be going and you must be
happy for me. By this time
tomorrow you will be a very happy
girl indeed, let me tell you. You
told me that you believed every
word I said. Believe me now.'

'All right,' said Harriet. She bent
and stroked his tawny back.

'Stroke my children when you
come upon them,' said the hare,
'and think of me.'

'I will, Wiz,' said Harriet. 'But I
don't want to say goodbye.'

'Then don't,' said the hare, and
with one easy bound he leaped over
the garden wall and was gone.

At the end of that first day of
September, Harriet stood at her
bedroom window, looking down
into the valley below and hoping

perhaps for one last glimpse of her hare, but there was no sign of him.

Already the full moon was sailing in the darkening sky, and Harriet stared up at it, thinking as she would now always think that that business of the Man in the Moon was rubbish. What was on the great round disc was, without a doubt, the outline of a hare.

Her father came in to say good-night.

'You haven't sold out of eggs, have you, Hat?' he asked.

'No. Why?'

'Might need an extra one for breakfast tomorrow.'

Greedy old Dad, Harriet thought, he never usually has two.

The night was a still one, and for some long time Harriet lay awake, straining her ears for any unusual sound. When she did at last fall asleep, she slept lightly, so that a distant noise woke her.

It was a rushing, tearing, swishing noise – just like the sound a rocket makes on Guy Fawkes Night, but this time it did not come from the valley below but from the opposite direction, far away, right up at the top of Longhanger Farm, up on the downs.

Harriet looked at her watch. It was midnight, the witching hour.

'Be happy for me,' he had said, she thought, so I must be, and she lay down again and shut her eyes.

When she opened them again it was to find that she had slept late. She went to the window and saw that her father had finished the morning milking, that the herd was already out at pasture, and that a car was coming up the trackway.

Jessica's car, thought Harriet. She must be out of eggs. And Harriet dressed quickly and ran downstairs.

Her father was already in the kitchen.

'Lay an extra place, will you, Hattie, please?' he called. 'Jessica's coming to breakfast,' and with that there was a knock on the front door.

'How d'you like your boiled egg, Jessica?' Harriet's father shouted from the kitchen.

'Sort of middling, please, John. Softish yolk, firmish white, if you know what I mean.'

'I do.'

'That's how we like ours,' said Harriet.

What's Jessica doing here for

breakfast? she thought. I mean, I'm glad she's here, I like her. Come to think of it I like her very much indeed. But why breakfast?

Not until they had finished eating did Jessica say, 'You're wondering why I'm here so early in the day, aren't you, Harriet? It's because I've got some news to tell you and I couldn't wait any longer.'

'Oh no!' cried Harriet. 'You're moving! Dad said you might be moving house.'

'Yes, I am. Not for some while yet, but then I shall sell the old turnpike cottage.'

'Where are you going to live then?' asked Harriet.

'At Longhanger Farm,' said her father.

Harriet looked blank. Her mind was still full of thoughts of Wiz, speeding away on his long long journey to Pars, and she could not grasp what was being said.

'Last Sunday,' said Jessica, 'after lunch when your father asked you to go and have a look at Buttercup, it was because he wanted to ask me something.'

'Over the washing-up,' said John Butler. 'Dead romantic.'

'He asked me to marry him, Harriet,' said Jessica Lambert, 'and I said, "Yes, but only if Harriet approves."'

Suddenly everything was blindingly clear to Harriet.

It was all Wiz's doing!

This was the good turn he'd promised. This was the really big surprise. He had arranged the whole thing, from the moment when he'd sat in the lane and caused

Jessica to go in the ditch, so that
Dad could rescue her.

'Tomorrow you will be a very
happy girl indeed,'
he had said
yesterday.
In fact, Harriet
was so delighted
that at first she
could not speak.
She jumped
up from the
table and

dashed round to Jessica and gave
her an enormous hug, and then she
gave her father another one.

At last she said, 'It's like a fairy-
tale.'

Jessica laughed.

'There's often a wicked
stepmother in a fairy-tale,' she said,
'but I'll try very hard to be a good
one. And I'll start by letting you off
the washing-up, Harriet. Or can I
call you Hattie too, now?'

'Whatever you like,' said Harriet
happily.

And she sat on by herself at the
breakfast table after they had
cleared it, and listened to the sounds
of talk and laughter coming from
the kitchen, and thought how
brilliant it was going to be for both
of them. For Jessica, after that
awful first husband who called her

'Jess' like a sheepdog and knocked her about, and for Dad, after almost six long, lonely years.

She stared up at the portrait hanging on the wall.

To Jessica, to her father, to Mrs Wisker or anyone else, it was just a very good likeness of a hare.

But to her and her alone, it was a portrait of a wizard – of a beast of magic who, for a thousand full moons to come, would remain, as he had always been, Harriet's hare.

THE END